19 Girls and Me

Darcy Pattison

ILLUSTRATED BY **Steven Salerno**

PHILOMEL BOOKS

PHILOMEL BOOKS

A division of Penguin Young Readers Group.

Published by The Penguin Group.

Penguin Group (USA) Inc., 375 Hudson Street, New York, NY 10014, U.S.A.

Penguin Group (Canada), 90 Eglinton Avenue East, Suite 700, Toronto, Ontario, Canada M4P 2Y3

(a division of Pearson Penguin Canada Inc.).

Penguin Books Ltd, 80 Strand, London WC2R 0RL, England.

Penguin Ireland, 25 St. Stephen's Green, Dublin 2, Ireland (a division of Penguin Books Ltd.).

Penguin Group (Australia), 250 Camberwell Road, Camberwell, Victoria 3124, Australia

(a division of Pearson Australia Group Pty Ltd).

Penguin Books India Pvt Ltd, 11 Community Centre, Panchsheel Park, New Delhi - 110 017, India.

Penguin Group (NZ), Cnr Airborne and Rosedale Roads, Albany, Auckland 1310, New Zealand

(a division of Pearson New Zealand Ltd).

Penguin Books (South Africa) (Pty) Ltd, 24 Sturdee Avenue, Rosebank, Johannesburg 2196, South Africa.

Penguin Books Ltd, Registered Offices: 80 Strand, London WC2R 0RL, England.

Published simultaneously in Canada. Manufactured in China by South China Printing Co. Ltd.
Design by Katrina Damkoehler. The text is set in Clair.
The illustrations were created with ink, watercolor, gouache and added digital enhancement.
Library of Congress Cataloging-in-Publication Data
Pattison, Darcy.   19 girls and me / Darcy Pattison ; illustrated by Steven Salerno.   p. cm.
Summary: John Hercules is worried about being the only boy in his
kindergarten class, but after the first week he stops worrying.
[1. Sex role—Fiction. 2. Play—Fiction. 3. Kindergarten—Fiction. 4. Schools—Fiction.]
I. Title: Nineteen girls and me. II. Salerno, Steven, ill. III. Title.
PZ7.P27816Aabj 2006   [E]—dc22   2005020501

ISBN 0-399-24336-4
1 3 5 7 9 10 8 6 4 2
First Impression

To Edith Elleen and Joyce Perry.
And to Rick:
Thanks for the loan of the ladder.—D.P.

For Laurie,
the best girl in the world.—S.S.

The kindergarten class in 9B was odd.

"Nineteen girls," said John Hercules Po. "And me."

John's big brother shook his head.

"Those girls are going to turn you into a sissy."

"Not me!" John Hercules said. "I'll turn those girls into tomboys."

At noon on Monday, the kindergarten went out.
John Hercules saw a long ladder near the wall.

"Let's climb Mount Everest!"

Nineteen girls and one lone boy,
they climbed and climbed.
They climbed so high,
they reached the Yeti's peak.

"Stay!" the Yeti cried. "Today, we play!"
Nineteen girls and one lone boy heaved
snowballs at the giant beast until—

"**Lunch!**" called Mrs. Ray.

Nineteen girls and one lone boy
warmed their hands with soup du jour.

"Nineteen tomboys," John Hercules said.
"They throw snowballs hard."
"Just wait," his brother said. "Those girls
will turn you into a sissy tomorrow."

At noon on Tuesday, the kindergarten went out.
John Hercules saw a shovel near the wall.

"Let's dig to China!"

Nineteen girls and one lone boy,
they dug and dug.
They dug so deep,
they reached the Great Wall.

In one lean line, they marched beside the sentry.
"I'm tired," Hannah Beth finally said.
"Could we have some tea?"
Nineteen girls and one lone boy
sipped green tea until—

"**Lunch!**" called Mrs. Ray.

Nineteen girls and one lone boy
used chopsticks to eat lo mein.

"Nineteen tomboys," John Hercules said.
"They dig fast." He didn't say anything about
the green tea or chopsticks.
"Digging is good," said John's brother,
"but be careful or those girls will turn you
into a sissy tomorrow."

At noon on Wednesday, the kindergarten went out.
John Hercules saw a water hose near the wall.

"Let's float down
the Amazon River!"

Nineteen girls and one lone boy, they paddled and paddled.
They paddled so fast, they ran right into a nest of alligators.
They wrestled and wrestled their way free.

"This rain forest has more than just alligators," Desiree Fai called.
"See?"

Nineteen girls and one lone boy
played hide-and-seek with
wild and freaky birds until—

"Lunch!" called Mrs. Ray.
Nineteen girls and one lone boy
ate fried piranha with ketchup.

"Nineteen tomboys," John Hercules said.
"They wrestle hard."
He didn't say anything about
the wild and freaky birds.
"Alligators are very good,"
John's brother said,
"but be careful or those girls will
turn you into a sissy tomorrow."

At noon on Thursday, the kindergarten went out.
John Hercules saw a hammer beside the wall.

"Let's build a skyscraper!"

Nineteen girls and one lone boy hammered and hammered.
They hammered until their skyscraper was high enough
that they could float over to the space station.

"Let's sing," Shayla Von said,
"to the Man in the Moon."
Nineteen girls and
one lone boy
sang atop the
gleaming moon until—

"Lunch!" called Mrs. Ray.

Uh-oh! The second-graders had already come out for recess.

John's brother had been watching them sing.

John Hercules ran over to his brother.

"Did you see us build a skyscraper?

We floated over to the space station."

"That part is good," said his brother.

"But singing to a Moon Man? Those girls got you today."

Nineteen girls ate tomato sauce with space worms.

But John Hercules didn't want to eat.

At noon on Friday, the kindergarten went out.
John Hercules saw a wagon beside the wall.

"Let's build a race car."

Nineteen girls and one lone boy
souped up the engine and raced and raced.
Faith Gish said, "Let's call our race car the *Sarah Louise*."
"That's a sissy name," John Hercules said.
"No," Faith Gish said, "that's my grandmother's name.
And besides, race car drivers always name their car after a girl."
"Oh. Okay," John Hercules said.

      Nineteen girls and one lone boy
         raced the *Sarah Louise* at six hundred
            miles an hour until—

"**Lunch!**" called Mrs. Ray.

She carried a large basket.

"The second-graders are going to picnic with us today."

John Hercules worried.

What would he tell his brother about the *Sarah Louise*?

The second-graders crowded around the souped-up wagon. "What is it?"

"Our race car," John Hercules said. "It just went six hundred and twenty-six miles an hour, a World Record!" "That's *good*," said John's brother. "No, SHE is good," John Hercules said.

He looked at the nineteen girls.
They had played fun games all week.
For every game, they had thought of
new ways to play it. He didn't care if
they were tomboys or if he was a sissy.
"We call our race car the *Sarah Louise*."
"You call it a girl's name?" asked John's brother.
John Hercules said proudly, "She's the best game in town."

"Can I ride in her?" asked a big second-grade boy.

"Yes," John Hercules said.

Then nineteen girls and one lone boy showed the second-graders how to heave snowballs at the Yeti.

They strolled atop the Great Wall of China and sipped green tea.

They wrestled
thirty-one
Amazon alligators,
and everyone played
hide-and-seek with wild
and freaky birds.

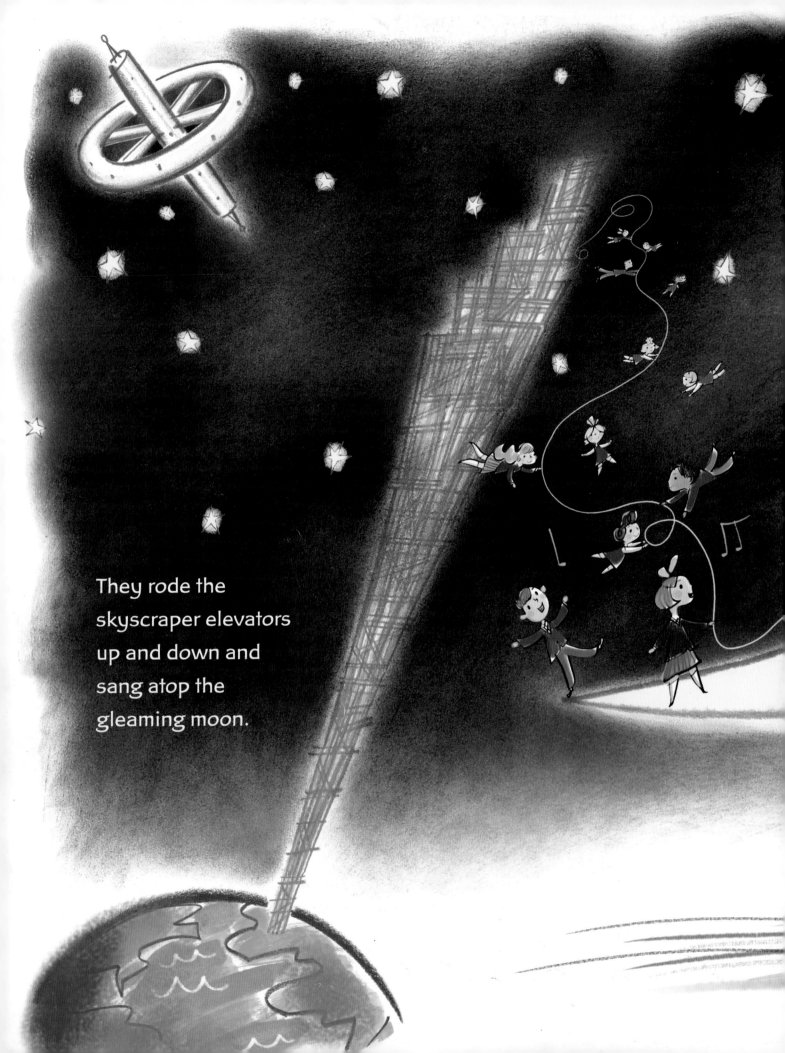

They rode the
skyscraper elevators
up and down and
sang atop the
gleaming moon.

They raced the *Sarah Louise* round and round
and ate cheeseburgers and chips.

At the end of recess, John's brother slapped him on the back.

"Nineteen tomboys. That's good."

"No," said John Hercules. "Nineteen friends."

And that was very good.